SCARED SILLY

STORIES TO MAKE YOU GASP AND GIGGLE

by **Judith Bauer Stamper**

Illustrated by **Tim Raglin**

Scholastic Reader — Level 4

SCHOLASTIC INC.

New York Toronto London Auckland Sydney
Mexico City New Delhi Hong Kong Buenos Aires

Five Funny Frights (978-0-590-46416-1)
Text copyright © 1993 by Judith Bauer Stamper.
Illustrations copyright © 1993 by Tim Raglin.

Five Creepy Creatures (978-0-590-92154-1)
Text copyright © 1997 by Judith Bauer Stamper.
Illustrations copyright © 1997 by Tim Raglin.

Five Haunted Houses (978-0-439-20546-7)
Text copyright © 2000 by Judith Bauer Stamper.
Illustrations copyright © 2000 by Tim Raglin.

Five Goofy Ghosts (978-0-590-92152-7)
Text copyright © 1996 by Judith Bauer Stamper.
Illustrations copyright © 1996 by Tim Raglin.

12 11 10 9 8 7 6 5 4   8 9 10 11 12 13/0

Printed in the U.S.A.   23
This edition created exclusively for Barnes & Noble, Inc.
2008 Barnes & Noble Books
ISBN-13: 978-0-7607-5682-9
ISBN-10: 0-7607-5682-1
This edition printing, August 2008

FIVE
FUNNY
FRIGHTS

by **Judith Bauer Stamper**
Illustrated by **Tim Raglin**

THE SKELETON

It was the scariest night
of the year.
Ben was waiting for his friend.
Where could he be?
Ben started to shiver.

A bat swooped down from a tree
right over Ben's head.
Ben almost jumped out of his skin.
Then he started to run.

Ben ran and ran until he couldn't
run anymore.
Finally, he stopped and sat down on
a cold, hard rock to rest.
Just then, the moon came out and lit
up the sky.

Ben looked down at the rock he was
sitting on.
It wasn't a rock at all.
It was a tombstone!
Ben looked around him.
He was sitting in the middle of
a cemetery!

From close behind him, Ben heard
a noise.
He turned around and saw a
skeleton.
It was coming right at him!
Ben jumped up and started to run for
his life.

He ran faster than he had ever
run before.
But the skeleton chased right
after him.
It was getting closer and closer.

Ben turned his head to look
behind him.
The skeleton was only a few
feet away.
It had a gruesome grin on its face.
Then it reached out a bony hand to
grab Ben.
But it just missed him!

By now, Ben was only one block
from his house.
He tried to run faster, but his legs felt
like jelly.
All of a sudden, he tripped on a tree
root and fell down to the ground.

Ben scrambled back to his feet as
fast as he could.
But the skeleton was right in front
of him.
Ben looked into his grinning face.
And he screamed!

Then the skeleton reached out a
bony hand.
It tapped Ben on the shoulder
And it said . . .

"TAG, YOU'RE IT!"

THE SCREAM

Jenny was staying with her
grandmother.
Her grandmother lived in a big old
house that had twenty-two rooms.
And people said it was full of ghosts.

One night, Jenny couldn't go
to sleep.
She tossed and turned and tossed
and turned in her bed.
She was thinking about the stories.
Did ghosts really live in
her grandmother's house?

Then, outside her door, Jenny heard
a strange noise in the hallway.
She pricked up her ears.
The noise sounded like soft
footsteps.
They were going
down the stairs.

Jenny became more and more curious.
Slowly, she crept out of bed.
She opened the door to her room.
She started to follow the footsteps down the stairs.

Finally, Jenny reached the bottom of the stairs.
She heard a soft moan come from down the hallway.
She tiptoed toward it in the dark.
The moaning sound moved toward the front door.
Then Jenny heard the door creak open.

She crept through the dark toward
the door.
Then she stepped out onto the big
porch in front of the house.
Another moan floated through
the air.
Jenny could tell it was from the steps
leading into the garden.
Slowly, she tiptoed down the steps.

For a minute, the moaning sound
stopped.
Jenny heard nothing but the sound
of the crickets in the night.
Then, from out in the garden,
the moaning started again.
Jenny stepped toward it over
the cold, soft ground.

Suddenly she screamed,
"AAAAAAAAAAAAAAAAAH!"

Well, you'd scream, too,
IF YOU STUBBED YOUR TOE ON
A ROCK!

A DARK, DARK STORY

In a dark, dark wood,
there was a dark, dark house.

And in that dark, dark house,
there was a dark, dark hall.
And in that dark, dark hall,
there was a dark, dark stairway.

And up that dark, dark stairway,
there was a dark, dark attic.

And in that dark, dark attic,
there was a dark, dark trunk.
And in that dark, dark trunk,
there was a dark, dark coat.

And in that dark, dark coat,
there was a dark, dark pocket.
And in that dark, dark pocket,
there was a dark, dark box.
And in that dark, dark box,
there was . . .

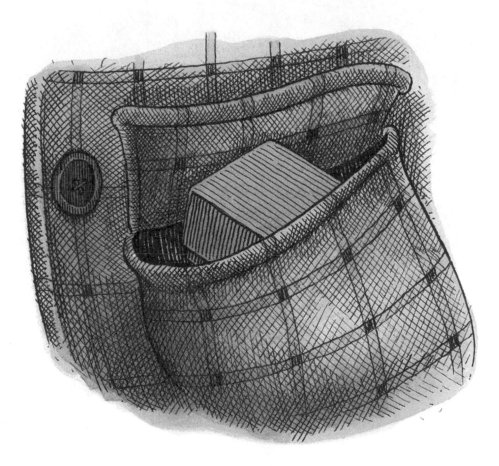

A PINK JELLYBEAN!

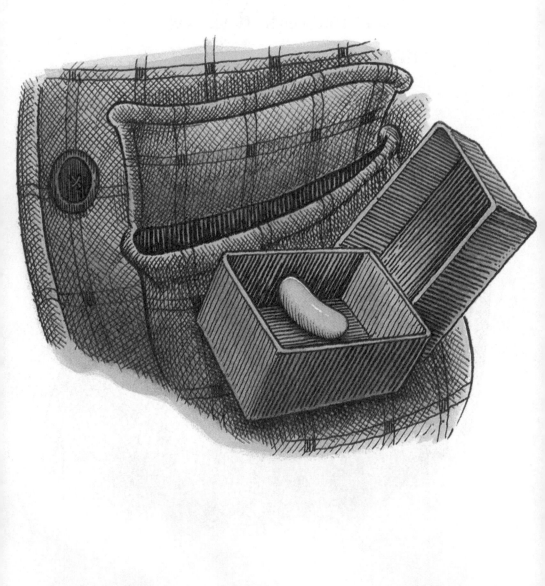

BLOODY FINGERS

Two brothers were camping out in
the woods.
They had gone on a long walk
through the tall, dark trees.
Now, they were lost.
The sun was sinking lower and lower
in the sky.

"I think camp is that way," one said.
"I think it's the other way," the
second said.
They stood looking at each other,
not knowing what to do.
Both of them were really scared.

Just then, they heard a sound behind
them.
Something was coming toward them
through the woods.
They turned around and looked.

It was a man, coming closer
and closer.
He was holding his hands up
in the air.
"Bloody fingers!" he called out
in a scary voice.

The two brothers looked at each
other with wide eyes.
Then they started to run.
The man ran after them.
"Bloody fingers!" he screamed.

The brothers ran faster and faster.
But the man kept up with them.
He held out his fingers.
They could see the blood!

"Bloody fingers!" the man kept
calling.
The boys were shaking with
fear now.
Then they saw their camp.
Maybe they could make it
to their tent!

The boys ran into the campground.
But the man kept right on running
after them.
"Bloody fingers!" he yelled.
He was getting closer and closer.

Just in time, the brothers ran into
their tent and hid under their cots.
Their mother and father were gone.
But their little sister was there.
Outside the tent, the man was still
screaming, "Bloody fingers!"

The little sister looked at her brothers
hiding under the cots.
Then she peeked through the tent
flap to look at the man.
"Bloody fingers!" he screamed
at her.

The girl picked up something from
a box in the tent.
Then she walked outside.
The man pointed his bloody fingers
at her.

"Bloody fingers!" he yelled.
"HAVE A BAND-AID!" she said.

GHOSTS!

One dark night, a boy was walking
home all alone.
Something about this night
made him feel afraid.

Suddenly rain came down in heavy
sheets.
The boy started to run.
He was still a long way from home.
And he had to find a dry place.

He ran down the road past an old
graveyard.
He looked over his shoulder at the
white tombstones, and ran even faster!
A short distance ahead was a big
barn in the middle of a field.
The barn looked old, but it would be
dry.

He pulled open the old barn door
and hurried inside.
He stood there, shivering.
The barn was dark but the boy found
a bale of hay and sat down on it.

A flash of lightning shot through the
sky.
For a second, it lit up the old barn.
The boy stared around him in shock.
Strange white shapes surrounded
him.

The boy screamed!
The ghosts must have followed him
from the graveyard!

Another flash of lightning lit the
barn.
The white shapes had moved closer
to him.
He jumped up from the bale of hay
and ran for the barn door.
But he tripped over one of the
ghosts!
"BAA-A-A!" it said.

The lightning flashed again.
The boy saw the white shapes clearly
for the first time.

FIVE CREEPY CREATURES

To my favorite creatures, Genevieve and Gwen
—J.B.S.

FIVE CREEPY CREATURES

by Judith Bauer Stamper • Illustrated by Tim Raglin

STOP THAT COFFIN!

One night, a boy took a walk
in a graveyard.
His little sister came along.
They walked along a path
lit by a big, yellow moon.
The boy was feeling scared.
But he acted cool and calm.

"I'm not afraid of graveyards,"
his sister said.
"You aren't?" the boy asked.
"Not a bit," his sister answered
with a smile.

They walked on past
the white tombstones.
Then they saw a big hole
dug in the ground.
"Dare you to look in that hole,"
his sister said.
"I'm not scared," the boy said
in a shaky voice.
"Then look in it," his sister dared.

The boy walked over to the hole.
His knees were shaking.
He inched up to the edge of the hole.
Then he looked in.

And a big, brown coffin
jumped out of the hole!
It started to chase the boy
and his sister.

They took off running.
But the coffin followed
right behind them!

BUMP! BUMP! BUMP!
The coffin bumped and jumped
along the cemetery path.
"We've got to get out of here!"
the boy screamed.
"I'm not afraid of that coffin,"
his sister said and laughed.

They ran until they reached the gates
of the graveyard.
They ran out onto the sidewalk.
"I think we lost it!" the boy said.

BUMP! BUMP! BUMP!
The coffin bumped and jumped
onto the sidewalk behind them.
"Run!" the boy screamed.
The coffin was so close
it was breathing down their necks!

The boy and his sister ran
until they reached their house.
They ran up the five front steps.
The coffin was right behind them.
BUMP! BUMP! BUMP!
That coffin jumped right up
those five steps.

The boy tried and tried to open
the front door.
But it was locked.
And there was the coffin!

His sister turned around
to stare at the coffin.
She reached in her pocket
and pulled out a box.
Then she took a cough drop out
and handed it to the coffin.
"This will stop that coffin!"
she said to her brother.

And the coffin stopped and went away.

WHO'S THERE?

KNOCK, KNOCK.

Who's there?

Weirdo.

Weirdo who?

Weirdo you think you're going?

KNOCK, KNOCK.
Who's there?
Horror.
Horror who?
Horror ya doing?

KNOCK, KNOCK.

Who's there?

Werewolf.

Werewolf who?

Werewolf I find a bathroom?

KNOCK, KNOCK.

Who's there?

Voodoo.

Voodoo who?

Voodoo you think you are?

KNOCK, KNOCK.

Who's there?

Boo.

Boo who?

Don't cry. I'm not going to eat you!

THE NEW NEIGHBOR

One hot, sleepy, summer day,
a new neighbor moved in.
Howard watched from his window.
The movers carried in a big, green chair.
Then they carried in a huge bed.
All day long, they carried in one thing
after another.

Howard watched and waited.
He wanted to see his new neighbor.
Finally, at midnight, a big, black car
pulled up to the house.
A dark figure got out and went into
the house.

Howard fell asleep.
He dreamed a long, weird dream
about the new neighbor.
He remembered it all the next morning.

"My new neighbor is a monster,"
he told his best friend.
"Don't tell anybody else."

Right away, the best friend told
another friend.

"Howard's new neighbor is a monster.
Don't tell anybody else."

That friend told her little brother.
"Howard's new neighbor is a monster.
Don't tell anybody else."

Soon, everyone in town knew
that Howard's new neighbor
was a monster.
No one wanted to go near the house.
Paperboys refused to deliver there.
Even the mailman ran to and from
the house.

Howard began to feel guilty.
He hadn't really seen his neighbor yet.
He had just *dreamed* he was a monster.
And now everyone was scared of him.
Howard knew it was wrong
to start a rumor.
He decided to apologize
to his new neighbor.

That night, he went to his neighbor's
house.
He knocked on the door.

No one came.

Howard started to get a little nervous.

But he had made up his mind.

He knocked on the door again.

Finally, he heard footsteps
coming toward the door.

But no one opened the door.

Howard called through the door,
"I'm sorry I called you a monster."

Then the door creaked open.

"That's all right,"
the new neighbor said.
"I am one!"

IN OLD TREES

In old trees,
there are holes
where the wood has rotted out.
But don't put your hand in to feel,
because . . .

In old trees,
there are holes
where the wood has rotted out,
and creatures live there
that no one sees.
But don't put your hand in to feel,
because...

In old trees,
there are holes
where the wood has rotted out,
and creatures live there
that no one sees.
They have yellow eyes and long noses
and sharp teeth.
But don't put your hand in to feel,
because . . .

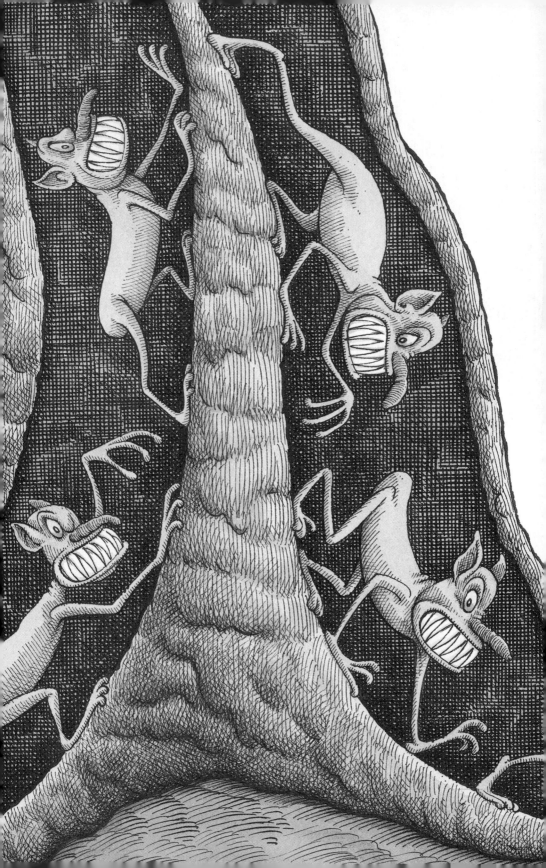

In old trees,
there are holes
where the wood has rotted out,
and creatures live there
that no one sees.
They have yellow eyes and long noses
and sharp teeth,
and they run up and down
and into the ground.
But don't put your hand in to feel,
because ...

In old trees,
there are holes
where the wood has rotted out,
and creatures live there
that no one sees.
They have yellow eyes and long noses
and sharp teeth,
and they run up and down
and into the ground.
And if you put your hand in to feel...

THEY'LL TICKLE YOU!

THE STRANGE VISITOR

Once there was a lonely, old woman
who lived in a house in the woods.
Each night, she sat by the fire
spinning her wool.
And so she sat.
And so she spun.
And so she waited
for someone to come.

One night, the door creaked open.
CREAK.
And in came —
a big pair of feet.

The feet stomped over to the fire
right beside the woman.
"How strange," the woman said.
And still she sat.
And still she spun.
And still she waited
for someone to come.

Then the door creaked open again.
CREAK.
And in came a pair of short,
hairy legs.
The legs sat themselves down
on the big feet.
"How strange," the woman said.
And still she sat.
And still she spun.
And still she waited
for someone to come.

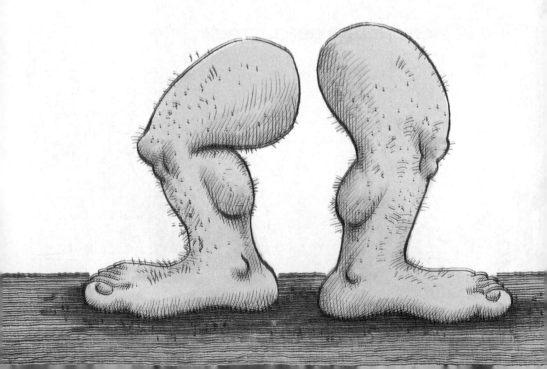

Once again, the door creaked open.
CREAK.
And in came a pair of huge hips.
The hips sat themselves down
on the short, hairy legs.
"How strange," the woman said.
And still she sat.
And still she spun.
And still she waited
for someone to come.

Then the door creaked open again.
CREAK.
And in came a broad chest and shoulders.
The chest and shoulders
sat themselves down on the huge hips.
"How strange," the woman said.
And still she sat.
And still she spun.
And still she waited
for someone to come.

Again, the door creaked open.
CREAK.
And in came a set of long arms
with fat fingers.
The arms and fingers
sat themselves down on the broad chest
and shoulders.
"How strange," the woman said.
And still she sat.
And still she spun.
And still she waited
for someone to come.

The door creaked open one more time.
CREAK.
And in rolled a huge, horrible head.

The head sat itself down
on top of the broad chest and shoulders.
"How strange," said the woman.

Then she asked, "How did you get
such big feet?"
"MUCH STOMPING. MUCH STOMPING,"
the visitor said.
"How did you get such short, hairy legs?"
"MUCH RUNNING. MUCH RUNNING."
"How did you get such huge hips?"
"MUCH EATING. MUCH EATING."
"How did you get such a broad chest
and shoulders?"
"MUCH FIGHTING. MUCH FIGHTING."
"How did you get such long arms
and fat fingers?"
"MUCH GRABBING. MUCH GRABBING."
"How did you get such a huge, horrible head?"
"MUCH THINKING. MUCH THINKING."

"Why did you come here?" the woman asked.
And the visitor replied . . .

"BECAUSE I NEED A HUG!"

FIVE GOOFY GHOSTS

by Judith Bauer Stamper · Illustrated by Tim Raglin

NEVER TALK TO A GHOST

Late one night, a boy took a walk.

His little dog went with him.

They walked down a lonely, dark lane.

"Wonder if we'll see a ghost?" the boy asked.

His little dog looked at him with big eyes.

They kept on walking down the lane.

The lane made a sharp turn to the left.

Then it came to a stop.

At the end was a big, old house.

"Let's go in," the boy said.
The little dog began to whimper.
He followed the boy to the door.

The old door creaked as it opened.
The boy stepped inside the house.
The dog followed close behind him.

"Anybody home?" the boy called out.
A moan came from up the stairs.
Then the lights went off and on.

"I wonder if it's a ghost?" the boy said.
Just then, the room got colder.
A ghost appeared on the stairs.

"Well, look at that!" the boy said.
The little dog hid behind the boy's legs.
The ghost moaned again.

"Ghosts don't scare me!" the boy said.
The ghost looked angry.
He floated right down the stairs.

"You should be scared!" the ghost said.
The boy started shaking all over.

Fast as he could, the boy ran out the door.
The little dog took off after him.
"I didn't know ghosts could talk," the boy said.

"Me, neither," the dog said. "Let's get out of here!"

A SCARY TALE

A brother and sister were visiting their grandmother.

She lived in a creepy, old house.

The brother and sister decided to explore.

They climbed up one flight of stairs.
The steps creaked and squeaked.

They climbed up another flight of stairs.
The steps creaked and squeaked.

They climbed up another flight of stairs.
They opened an old door.
It creaked and squeaked.

The brother and sister walked into an old attic.
It was filled with boxes and trunks.
Cobwebs were everywhere.

"This is creepy!" the sister said.
"You're a fraidy-cat," the brother said.
"No, I'm not."
"Yes, you are!"

The sister got mad at her brother.
She wanted to prove that she wasn't a
fraidy-cat.
She looked around and found an old sheet.
She put it over her head.

Then she hid behind a big trunk.
Her brother walked by.
She jumped out and yelled, "Boo!"

Her brother stared at her.
His hair was standing on end.

"It's only me," the sister said.
"I know," her brother said.

THE TRUNK FULL OF TREATS

This is the trunk full of treats.

This is the bat, big and brown,
That's fast asleep, upside down,
Over the trunk full of treats.

This is the skeleton, bony and white,
Waiting in the attic to give you a fright,

If you bother the bat, big and brown,
That's fast asleep, upside down,
Over the trunk full of treats.

This is the witch with long, black hair,
Who rocks all night in her squeaky chair,

Beside the skeleton, bony and white,
Waiting in the attic to give you a fright,
If you bother the bat, big and brown,
That's fast asleep, upside down,
Over the trunk full of treats.

These are the monsters who sit in a bunch,
Moaning and groaning as they munch
and crunch,

Around the witch with long, black hair,
Who rocks all night in her squeaky chair,
Beside the skeleton, bony and white,
Waiting in the attic to give you a fright,
If you bother the bat, big and brown,
Fast asleep, upside down,
Over the trunk full of treats.

This is the zombie who walks with a thump,
All night you can hear him clumpety-clump.

He guards the monsters who sit in a bunch,
Moaning and groaning as they munch
and crunch,
Around the witch with long, black hair,
Who rocks all night in her squeaky chair,
Beside the skeleton, bony and white,
Waiting in the attic to give you a fright,
If you bother the bat, big and brown,
That's fast asleep, upside down,
Over the trunk full of treats.

This is the ghost who scared the zombie away,

And tickled the monsters and told them to play,

And shooed away the witch on her ragged broom,

And sent the skeleton back to his tomb,

And chased off the bat, big and brown,

And pulled off his sheet and sat himself down,

And opened the trunk full of treats!

THE HAIRY TOE

Once there was a girl who was very curious.
This girl liked to hunt around for strange things.
In fact, she had a collection of strange things.

She had a snake's skin.
She had a toad's skeleton.
She had a piece of furry moss.
She had lots of other strange things, too.

One day, the girl passed by an old house.
A ghost was supposed to live in this house.
The girl went in anyway, just to look.
And what did she find?
A hairy toe!

"Wow!" the girl said. "A hairy toe for
my collection."
She picked up the hairy toe and ran home.
She set it on the table with her collection.

That night, the girl fell asleep right away.
But a voice woke her in the middle of the night.
"Who-o-o-o's got my hairy toe?"

The girl felt a shiver creep over her.
She pulled her blanket higher over her chin.
Then she heard the voice again, closer.
"Who-o-o-o's got my hairy toe?"

The girl could see the hairy toe on the table.
It seemed to be shining in the moonlight.
Then a cold breeze swept through the room.
And she heard the voice again, louder.
"Who-o-o-o's got my hairy toe?"

A white shape moved across the room.
The girl knew it was the ghost.
She trembled underneath the covers.
The ghost came closer and closer.
"Who-o-o-o's got my hairy toe?"

The girl jumped out of bed and ran for the table.
She picked up the hairy toe.
"Take it!" she yelled.
She threw the hairy toe at the ghost.

The ghost ran away with his hairy toe.
"Oh, goodie!" he said. "I've got my hairy
toe back!"

And the girl never saw him again.

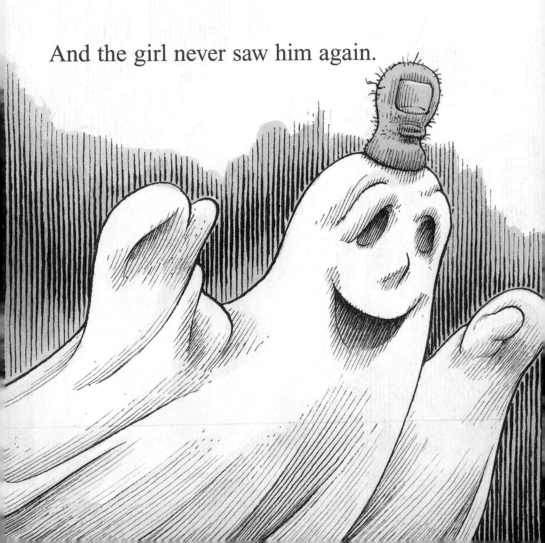

THE LAST LAUGH

Two boys sat on an old stone wall.
Behind them was a graveyard.

"Do you know what the little ghost wore on
Halloween?" one boy asked.
"A pillowcase."

The boys laughed so hard they almost fell off the wall.

"Where do ghosts go to retire?" the other boy asked.
"A ghost town."

The boys laughed and laughed.

"How did the little ghost do his homework?" the first boy asked.
"He hired a ghostwriter."

The boys laughed so loud their voices echoed in the graveyard.

"Where did the ghost keep his rock collection?" the second boy asked.
"In a graveyard."

The boys laughed and slapped their knees.

"What did the ghost say to the two boys?"
the ghost asked.

"Boo!"

For Virginia Bauer,
my warm and wonderful mother
—J.B.S.

FIVE HAUNTED HOUSES

by Judith Bauer Stamper • Illustrated by Tim Raglin

ARE YOU AFRAID OF GHOSTS?

High on a hill sat an old house.
Its windows were broken.
Its shutters creaked.
Bats flew in and out of the chimney.

Kids walked faster when they passed by it.
Everyone said it was a haunted house.
Everyone but Jake.
Jake didn't believe in ghosts.

One night, Jake and his friend
walked by the house.
His friend wanted to run.
Jake stopped right in front.
"Are you coming in with me?" he asked.
"Not me!" his friend said.
Then he took off running.
"Chicken!" Jake yelled after him.

Jake stood on the sidewalk all alone.
He looked up at the house.
A big full moon shone down on it.
Jake felt a shiver creep up his spine.

"I'm not afraid of ghosts!" Jake said
to himself.
Then he walked right up to the house.
He knocked on the door three times.
KNOCK! KNOCK! KNOCK!

The door swung right open.
Jake peeked inside. Nobody was there,
so he walked on in.

Jake went into the living room.
The only light was from the fireplace.
Everything looked dark and shadowy.

Jake went up to a big chair
in front of the fireplace.
He sat down.
Then he just about jumped out of his skin!

A girl was sitting in the chair
just across from him.
She smiled at Jake.
"What's wrong?" she asked.
"Are you afraid?"

"I'm not afraid of anything," he said.
"Me neither," said the girl.

"My friends are afraid of this house,"
Jake said. "But I'm not."
"Me neither," said the girl.

Jake frowned.
This girl had to be afraid
of something.
Maybe he could scare her.

"Everyone says this house is haunted,"
Jake said. "But I'm not afraid of ghosts."
"Me neither," said the girl.

Then she smiled at Jake.
And disappeared.

YOU'LL BE SORRY

Lisa was visiting her aunt and uncle.
They lived in an old house
filled with strange things.
Some people said the house was haunted.
But Lisa didn't care.
She liked scary stuff.

She liked the fireplace that threw
scary shadows on the wall.

She liked the tall windows that rattled
like bones in the wind.

She liked the winding staircase that had
old, creaky steps.

Most of all, she liked the marble statue
at the bottom of the staircase.

The statue was of an old man.

His marble face was set in an awful frown.

In his twisted hands he held a handkerchief.

The weirdest thing was, he wore a pair of

thick, wool socks over his marble feet.

Lisa wondered what was under

those wool socks.

"Can I take off his socks?" Lisa asked

her uncle.

"You'll be sorry if you do," her uncle said.

"So don't!"

Lisa passed the statue every time she went
up and down the stairs.
She was dying to find out what was under
those socks!

Lisa looked around. She reached out to
touch the socks.
Just then, her aunt came by.
"Can I take off his socks?" Lisa asked
her aunt.
"You'll be sorry if you do," her aunt said.
"So don't!"

That night, Lisa went up to her bedroom.
She pretended to go to sleep.
But instead, she waited until the house was
dark and quiet.
Then she crept down the stairs.

The statue waited for her at the bottom of
the steps.
It was lit by moonlight coming in from
a window.
Lisa looked at its frowning face.
She looked at its twisted hands.
Then she looked down at the socks.
Finally, she would find out what was
under them!
Her hands trembled as she reached out
for the socks.
Then, quickly, she pulled both socks off.

"EEEEEWWWW!!!!" Lisa screamed.
Under the socks were two ... horrible ...

SMELLY FEET!

A TERRIBLE FRIGHT!

Five little ghosts
lived in a haunted house.

"EEEK!" said the first.
"I just saw a mouse!"

"Help!" said the second.
"There's a spider on the wall!"

"Yikes!" said the third.
"A bat is in the hall!"

"Yuck!" said the fourth.
"There's a lizard on the floor."

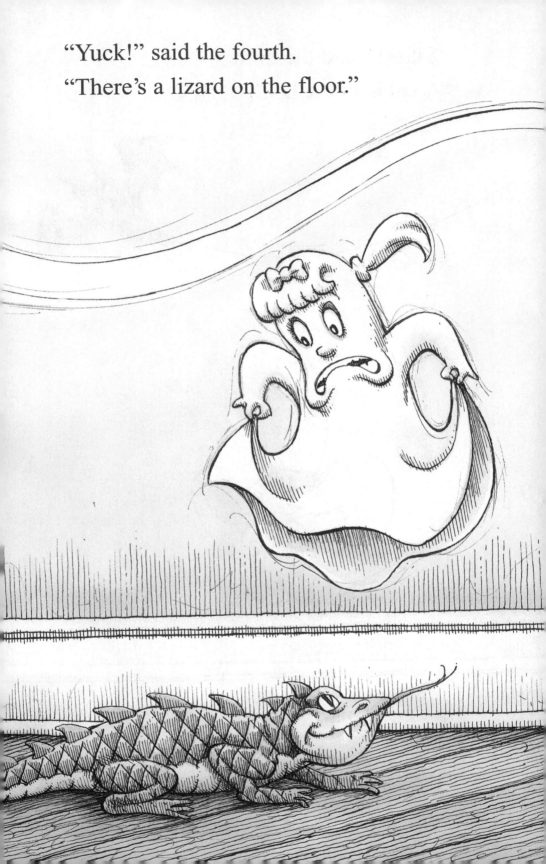

"Uh-oh!" said the fifth.

"I hear a knocking on the door."

Then . . . *Ooooooo* went the wind,
and out went the light.

And the five little ghosts
got a terrible fright!

RAP, RAP, RAP!

Luis couldn't believe his eyes.
His new house was a nightmare!
And his family was moving in
that very night.

Luis followed his mother and father
up to the house.
The front steps creaked and moaned.
His father opened the door.
It creaked and groaned.
They all walked inside.

Luis looked around.

The inside was just as bad as the outside.

Old. Dusty. Dark.

And creepy!

"I won't live here," Luis said to his mother
and father.

They just smiled and patted his head.

"You'll get used to it, Luis," they said.

Luis climbed the stairs to his bedroom.
His footsteps echoed through the house.
He kept stopping to look around.
Was something following him?

Luis went straight into his room.

He jumped right into bed.

He turned off the light.

Then he pulled the sheet up over his head.

Everything was quiet... as quiet as a tomb.
Then Luis heard a sound.
It went...
RAP! RAP! RAP! TAP! TAP! TAP!
And something pulled the sheet off
Luis's bed!

"EEEEEEKKKKKK!!!!!!!"
Luis screamed his head off!

Luis's mother and father came running.
They put his sheet back on him.
They sang him songs.
They told him it was just a bad dream.
But Luis knew better!

The next night, Luis climbed the stairs to his bedroom.

His footsteps echoed through the house.

He kept stopping to look around.

Was something following him?

Luis went straight into his room.

He jumped right into bed.

He turned off the light.

Then he pulled the sheet up over his head.

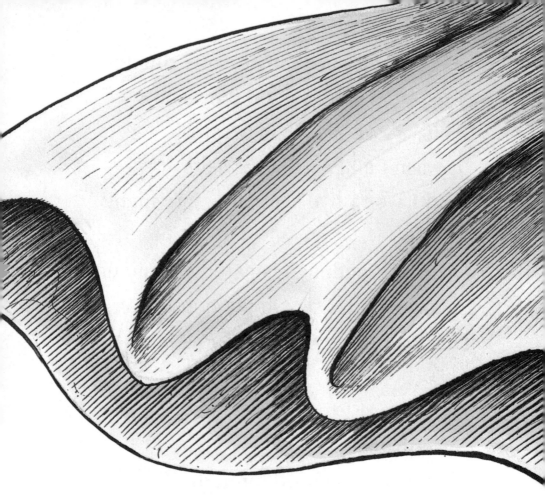

Everything was quiet... as quiet as a grave.

Then Luis heard a sound.

It went...

RAP! RAP! RAP! TAP! TAP! TAP!

And something pulled the sheet off
Luis's bed!

"EEEEEKKKKKKK!!!!"
Luis screamed his head off again.

Luis's mother and father came running.

"Luis, stop screaming!" they said.

"You've just had a bad dream."

"It wasn't a dream," Luis said.

"And I won't live here one more night!"

There was nothing his parents could do.

Luis would not stay in the house.

They had to pack up and move.

The next day, Luis carried all his things

down the staircase.

His footsteps echoed through

the empty house.

He kept stopping to look around.

Was something following him?

Luis put all his things in the trunk.
Then he got into the backseat of the car.
Luis watched the house as they drove away.
He never wanted to see that house again!

Everything was quiet in the car...as quiet as a coffin.

Then Luis heard a sound coming from the trunk.

It went...

RAP! RAP! RAP! TAP! TAP! TAP!

And a little voice whispered into Luis's ear...

"So, where are we going?"

THE GREEN DOOR

It was Halloween, the spookiest night of
the year!
Tom couldn't wait to go trick-or-treating.
This year, he was dressing up as a vampire.

Tom put fangs on his teeth.
He painted his face white.
He threw a black cape around his shoulders.
Then he got his bag for treats.

Tom went to meet his friend Ben.
Ben had just moved to an old house.
It sat on the edge of town.
Tom had not been there yet.
But he knew it had a green door.

Tom walked along the streets.
The night was very dark.
A full moon was in the sky.

Everyone was out trick-or-treating.
Monsters. Mummies. Vampires. Witches.
Tom felt a little afraid.
He couldn't wait to get to Ben's house.

He walked and walked to the edge of town.
All the houses were old and gloomy.
Then he saw it ... the house with the
green door.
He walked up and rang the doorbell.

A monster opened the door.
"Hi, Ben," Tom said.
A noise came out of the monster's mouth.
It sounded like, "GRUMF."
"Are you ready to go trick-or-treating?"
Tom asked.
"GRUMF!" the monster answered.
"I like your costume," Tom said.
"GRUMF!" the monster answered.

The two friends went from house to house.
"Trick-or-treat!" Tom said.
"GRUMF!" the monster answered.

Their treat bags got fuller and fuller.
"I love Halloween," Tom said.
"GRUMF!" the monster answered.

They went up to the next house.

It was old.

It had a green door.

Tom rang the doorbell.

"Trick-or-treat!" he yelled.

Ben opened the door.

"Where have you been?" Ben asked.

Tom's eyes got bigger and bigger.
He turned around.
"GRUMF!" answered the monster.

Then it ran off into the night.